Shilling for the Gate

Mary John

Illustrations by
Bryan Jones

Pont Books

First Impression—1991

ISBN 0 86383 763 8

© Mary John

This novel was commissioned by the Welsh Arts Council and was first published in 1990 in Welsh as *Swllt i'r Glwyd,* under the auspices of the WJEC's Welsh Readers Scheme as part of the Welsh History Project.

The publishers acknowledge the help and assistance of the Editorial Department of the Welsh Books Council which is supported by the Welsh Arts Council.

Printed by
J. D. Lewis & Sons, Ltd., Gomer Press, Llandysul, Dyfed.

1

Beti hurried down the long, straight avenue between the elms towards the main gates. Kitchen maids were expected to use the wicket gate in the garden wall on the far side of the Tŷ Mawr estate, but she really was very late going home and there would be few people about to notice her. Mrs Wynne-Jones' guests had lingered long over their afternoon tea and there had been a call for more ham sandwiches and extra helpings of Cook's gooseberry tart which meant more plates and more washing-up for Beti when the tea trolleys were finally wheeled back into the scullery.

'Hey!'

Beti was so startled she nearly dropped the basket she was carrying. It was only her friend Jenkyn Griffiths, the gardener's son, weeding a distant rose-bed. 'Naughty girl, Beti!' he called, a grin spreading over his face.

She waved back and hurried on. The gates which should have been closed behind the carriage of the last departing guest, were still standing wide. What a relief not to have to battle against the heavy wrought iron with her aching arms and her hands still red raw from scraping and scrubbing. As she crept through, Beti prayed that old Daniels was still snoozing in his lodge. Then, with a sigh she turned away from the drive onto a track running east across the top of the hills and towards home.

They'd be waiting for her, the little ones, anxious to search her basket. Today Cook had said she could take the last slice of gooseberry tart and a very small ham bone. Because she worked at the Big House it was assumed at home that she was well-fed but there were many times when she walked this way with just a few hastily snatched scraps inside her. This was one of those times. Resisting the temptation to scoff the gooseberry tart by picturing the faces of her little brothers, she stepped out briskly in the evening sun which was now casting her long shadow before her.

Beti had not gone far along the path before she realised something very strange was happening. Her shadow had suddenly grown much bigger, sometimes looking like a great hooded figure, hurrying ahead when she quickened her pace, slowing when she slowed and sometimes dividing into two shadows, both going along together. Her heart thumped. She was tired and she couldn't make sense of it. She felt compelled to stop and then at once a voice, deep and yet harsh, spoke up from behind her.

'Beti, Beti! No, don't look round! Just take

this message to your father, Gwilym Roberts of Pencnwc. Tell him to meet Rebecca by the valley gate at sunset this night, on horseback, with torch and axe!'

That was all. A silence and a scuffling on the grass. Then Beti turned and saw a figure in bonnet and shawl scrambling through the bushes on the slope below, petticoats catching in the brambles.

Beti knew what it meant. This was the message her father had expected all summer, the call from Rebecca, the words her stepmother feared because it threatened her husband's job as a carter and a smallholder, his life even. It could mean they would all go more hungry than ever.

She hurried on home to Pencnwc, the low cottage of stone and thatch, in view now, crouching among the rocks on the next ridge. Down below on the road to town stood the tollgate and the gatekeeper's house, the neat, six-sided white home of Twm Turnpike, Sarah Davies, his wife, and their little girl, Mari. Had they any idea what was going to happen tonight?

The family had already started on the potato broth when Beti entered the one-roomed cottage. The bone at once joined the potatoes simmering in the black pot over the fire, and with anxious joy the little ones watched their

8

privileged elder brother, Dewi, draw the glistening gooseberry tart from the basket. Their father had finished his broth and was rolling his tongue around his lips, but before he could reach for the tart Beti spoke up.

'Someone stopped me with a message for you, Da.'

'What message?'

'She said to be at the gate at sunset.'

'Hush!' Gwenno, her stepmother, rose with a clatter from the table, grabbed the first empty plate that came to hand, attacked the contents of the burbling pot with the ladle and set a meagre portion of broth before Beti.

Gwilym Roberts frowned but remained in his seat across the table, his face cupped in his hands.

'When was this?' he murmured.

'Just now, half way home.'

'A big woman?'

Beti nodded. Her stepmother, placing herself behind Gwilym's chair, angrily drew in her breath, 'Rebecca!'

'You can't be sure.'

'Of course it's Rebecca! Who else?'

'A trick. It could be a trick!'

'A trick? Whatever for? Tell me the message again, Beti. Every word mind.'

As she repeated it, Beti found herself stumbling over the words and she feared they

9

might think she was making it up. The meeting on the hill now began to seem so unreal.

'So! It's our turn at last. It had to come!' Her father sighed.

'You say that! But they can't destroy all the gates. Why the valley gate? Why ours?' Gwenno looked round wildly at her family, the four tired faces of the boys, propping each other up on the bench against the wall, and baby Catrin now curled sucking her fingers on Beti's lap. Gwenno's hands pressed into her plump belly where yet another new life was being prepared.

'Why can't we be left alone? How do they think we manage?'

'That's exactly it!' Gwilym bawled. 'Rebecca and her daughters destroy the gates because people like us shouldn't have to pay so much to go through them! Shouldn't have to pay at all! Bring back the old days when parish folk turned out to mend their own roads! These big men with money taking over, putting up gates every few miles! Making us pay, just to take our goods to town, and the roads no better than they were in the old days! Making a profit out of us! As if times aren't hard enough with tithes and taxes and low wages!'

'Will you go tonight then, Da?' Beti enquired in a voice barely above a whisper.

'No, indeed he will not!' her stepmother snapped. 'Get these children to their beds, Beti. And you can stay up there with them while your father and I talk this out in private.'

This was Beti's job every night, no matter how late she returned home. Often her father would fetch the loft ladder which for lack of space was left outside against the pine end wall, but not this night. While the three eldest boys devoured the gooseberry tart between them and then climbed the ladder, Beti put the baby to sleep in the cot alongside her parent's box bed and then carried the next smallest up to the loft in her arms and laid him down with the others on the great feather mattress amongst the straw. There was room enough for them all, including herself, on the mattress and they each had a piece of flannel to cover them.

For a long time the mattress creaked and the straw rustled as the little ones rolled and shuffled about. Beti was able to hear only snatches of conversation between her parents below, but as the children settled into sleep her stepmother's voice seemed to grow more shrill.

'You promised me, Gwilym, you wouldn't get involved!'

'What choice have I got?'

'Send Beti down. Tell them you're not well.'

11

'They're not going to believe that! Besides the child's fast asleep.'

'If it means keeping this family out of trouble we must try anything. Do you want to see us turned out of this cottage because we helped Rebecca? You in the county goal, me and the children in the workhouse!'

'Look. Every day I cart goods into market I'm paying that toll, me and every other farmer and carter in West Wales, for that matter. While the members of the Toll Trusts get fat on the takings, we're being crippled. We're only a spit away from the workhouse now. Can't you see? Rebecca is making a protest. She wants us all to stand together. It's high time those gates were destroyed, every last one of them! That's all they're doing, Gwen, demanding justice!'

'But smashing down gates! Burning tollhouses! Threatening the gatekeepers. There's a wife and child in that house, Gwilym!'

Beti heard her father's chair scraping on the stone flags. He was preparing to go.

'Gwilym!'

'Think, Gwenno! Do you imagine Rebecca will let us sleep easy in our beds if I do not go with her tonight? No. When it comes to it there's no choice. If it eases your mind I'll turn Blod into the pasture, tell them there was no

12

catching her in the dark. I'll be on foot, less obvious. Have you a shawl for me?'

'Get your own shawl! You'll need more than that to disguise you. You great hulk!'

Beti heard the latch raised. A rush of cool air invaded the cottage and the door closed firmly behind her father as he went out into the night. Shortly afterwards she could hear her stepmother sobbing.

2

Many times like this since she was very small Beti had pushed her way through the tiny window below the gable and, climbing through the dense branches of the yew tree against the wall, had let herself down to the ground. People who lived on meagre fare in the hillside cottages grew neither too broad nor too fat to climb through tight holes and narrow spaces. The heat of the summer day still lingered and there was just light enough for her to find her footing under the clear night sky, glowing apple green over the hills of Wales.

Barefoot she padded through the dewy grass, saving her clogs until she was clear of the cottage and for the prickly path between the gorse. She had walked this way so often in

13

darkness she had no fear of the black shadows.

There were noises about though; a far-off fox barking, badgers snuffling along the banks, and then others she thought she heard; distant hoofs on the road between the hills, urgent voices, a man calling, perhaps her father.

Beti ran, forcing her tired legs on, guided by the pinprick of light which grew bigger the nearer she came to the slope overlooking the tollhouse, and she became aware of a blazing column below her on the valley road moving along with her.

Someone was there before her, doing what she had come to do, watching from the hill. It was Harri from the Big House and he looked very startled when she first appeared out of the darkness.

'Beti, look! Down there! The road's lit up for miles!'

'What are you doing here?' she demanded. The hills were her territory. Harri belonged behind the walls of the estate. He was a year older than Beti. All the time she had lived in the cottage, Harri had lived in the Big House, but they were strangers because they did not see each other and just at the time Beti was old enough to help out at the Big House Harri was old enough to be sent away to school in England. Now, during the holidays, she would see him wandering in the garden or in the

rooms of the house alone, fed-up and generally ignoring her. After all she was only a kitchen maid.

He ignored her question now but he was excited and unusually anxious to talk.

'I've been watching them for ages. There must be hundreds of people down there!'

Even as he spoke the sound of their tramping and their bursts of chanting rose up the hill and Beti, looking down on the snaking, torchlit column, waited for Harri to ask if she knew what was happening, but he said nothing, which made her uneasy. Was it possible for a boy to know that Rebecca and her daughters would be out tonight when he lived shut away in Tŷ Mawr with no friends, with his mother only interested in parties and new gowns and a haughty grandfather locked in his study?

'It's a sitting duck tonight,' said Harri.

He was right, of course. There were lamps in every window of the tollhouse, casting light onto the great white, offending gate which barred the way on the road to town and flooding the wall where hung the white board with its hateful toll charges painted black. Beti thought she could see faces at the upstairs window. They must be able to see the glow and hear the noise. The column was only a few hundred yards from the gate. She would have

16

wanted to get out of that house quickly. What chance would they stand against so many?

'Your father's down there, I suppose,' said Harri.

Beti froze.

'Is that why you're here to watch?' he asked in a very matter of fact way. 'Oh look! They've stopped!'

Back up the road the crowd halted in silence though the torches burned more fiercely than ever, and the smell of pitch drifted on the breeze up the hill to where Beti and Harri waited for their next move. Then, they heard a thud in the tollhouse followed by a grating sound and the tollkeeper's door opened wide. Twm Davies emerged with a lantern in one hand and a stick in the other. Beti watched him take a few brisk paces into the road. He was checking the gate, probably for the hundredth time that night. He stood out in the open for what seemed like endless minutes in that desperate quiet, looking towards the flickering lights, listening. Then quickly he went inside and bolted the door and very soon the whole tollhouse was plunged into darkness.

'Now what?' muttered Harri, breathing hard and tramping about excitedly in the undergrowth. 'Ouch! I've been bitten!'

Beti guessed he had strayed into the gorse. She kept quiet, hoping he'd decide to go home, but at that moment something started up below. A lone horse was cantering towards the tollgate and as it rounded the bend in the road Beti could see on its back a figure in a flowing white gown.

Rebecca!

As the horse pulled up short at the gate a voice rang out. 'Children, there is something put up here. I cannot go on!'

A great roar rose from the crowd still holding back along the road, 'What is it, Mother? Nothing should block your way!'

'It seems like a great gate placed across the road to stop your old mother. Off with it then, my dear children! It has no business here.'

'That's not a woman!'

Harri's voice was drowned by the response of the crowd. It was the last thing he said to her that night for amid the sound of gunshot the horde rushed forward and the attack on the tollgate began.

Within seconds the shouting crowd had hacked the gate to pieces with their axes and hammers and the gateposts with it, and a torch was put to the pile of wood. Then they danced and sang around the blaze in their petticoats and shawls and shouted to the gatekeeper to come out now and to show his face. The

19

clamour went on and on but the house remained in darkness.

Beti shuddered. Where was her father in all this? Was that him leaping by the fire? Or was he one of the few still hanging back in the shadows? The white tollgate, dying in flames, glinted in the windows of the tollhouse as the daughters of Rebecca continued their rampage. They wrenched the tollboard from the wall of the house and sent it crashing onto the fire. Sparks flew high and wide, up onto the roof of the house where a few shreds caught in the eaves, flickered into life and very soon began a blaze which spread below the slates.

'The house is on fire!' A roar of delight rose up when the crowd saw what Beti had seen but when a child was heard screaming and as one by one lights appeared at the tollhouse windows, the excitement died away. Then the tollhouse door opened and Twm Davies appeared out of the smoke with his wife and child, and as the family escaped Twm's cry came out of the night. 'The Lord forgive you, Rebecca, for this night's work! I shall not!'

'Your forgiveness is not required, Twm Davies, tolltaker! It is we who will come to forgive you the evil tolls you have taken from your fellows round about! Let there be an end to it. Or you will suffer more than you have suffered here this night! Away, my daughters!'

Rebecca hurled her challenge and cantered off and the jeering crowd melted back into the night. Beti watched the farmers and carters and smallholders swinging their lamps and torches, their axes and hammers back down the road until the pinpricks of light dispersed far and wide into the dark lanes and fields.

The tollgate and the tollboard had burnt down to embers. Mercifully the blaze on the tollhouse roof was reluctant to spread and a few guilty souls stayed behind to drench the roof with water from the brook. Soon there was nothing left to witness, just the occasional whiff of smoke and a stray voice in the darkness.

'Twm Davies, come home! Twm Davies, come home!'

Time to go home. Beti's head throbbed. She could hardly credit what she had seen. For confirmation she turned to Harri. He'd gone. She was alone and very tired.

She picked her way back along the path towards home wondering if her stepmother had missed her. It was unlikely. Gwenno did not notice her much anyway, not when there were all the little ones to think about. Beti had never allowed herself to be upset by this fact. She supposed it must be very much the same for Harri. His mother did not notice him either. Except, perhaps, to notice that his boot laces were undone or his hair needed brushing before her guests arrived!

Why had he gone off like that? And how would he get back into Tŷ Mawr? It was a wonder they had not sent out a search party. Men with dogs! Beti shivered. The Daughters of Rebecca had left behind them a chill, friendless night. Pale, fluttering candlelight from the window of Pencnwc was her only guide past the pigsty where the sow still snuffled and up the path through the peas and beans. She had just found the yew tree and was slipping her feet from her clogs when a light appeared on the side of the hill. Someone was out there with a lantern.

'That you, Da?'

'Beti! What are you doing out here in the dark?'

'I came out to watch.'

Her father came up close to her, breathing heavily. By the light of his lantern she could see his face blacked up with soot and there was an old sack round him. He didn't look like a woman though, more like a demon, some wild thing with staring eyes and gaping mouth that had just done things he'd not likely forget.

'You saw all that?' He gripped her arm fiercely. 'You may wish you hadn't, child! We may all rue this night.'

22

'Gwenno's right then, about us being in trouble.'

'You've too sharp an ear for your own good!' her father retorted and pushed her hard towards the door.

3

That night Beti dreamed her home was on fire, that she woke to find crackling straw and the little ones coughing as the flames leaped around the mattress. Sparks were flying up to the sloping rafters and through the swirling smoke she heard her father calling. 'What's up, Beti?'

Beti opened her eyes and discovered she was looking into the light of a candle.

'What's up, girl?' Gwilym was at the top of the loft ladder with his night-light and she was lying stiff and cold on the mattress with her brothers awake and kneeling wide-eyed around her.

'Just a bad dream,' she explained.

'Aye, and enough to wake the whole household,' snapped her father. 'That's what comes of wandering the hills after dark, seeing things you shouldn't see. Now look, the baby's crying.'

It took a while for the family to settle back to sleep and Beti dozed only fitfully until daylight when she was disturbed by her youngest brother, little Rhys, pulling the end of a feather through the mattress. She picked him up and, leaving the others still asleep, took him down the ladder. At once tight-lipped Gwenno pulled him away from her and smothered the child with kisses.

'Might as well have your father's buttermilk. I'll not see it wasted.'

'Where is he?' Beti yawned.

'Not here. That's for sure. Sneaked out, like you did last night, my girl!' Gwenno rattled the embers of last night's fire and threw on some ash twigs which spat at them as they caught. 'Whatever it was you saw last night, you'll be sorry! I could be very thankful you're not my daughter!'

Beti gasped. With shaking hands she returned the wooden bowl to the table, opened the door to the misty morning and in a daze walked round the side of the cottage to the pump. She worked the pump handle to make the water spurt out icy cold into the bucket and cupping her hands splashed it to her face. Wide awake now and shivering she was ready for her walk to Tŷ Mawr. Back inside the cottage she ignored her unkind stepmother, made a big fuss of kissing all the children, smoothed

24

and pinned back her black hair, picked up her shawl and her basket and set off with an embittered heart.

Anyone would think she had been down there herself, attacking that gate!

'I'm not one of Rebecca's daughters,' Beti announced to the mist, 'and I'm not your daughter either, Gwenno!' She could only suppose her stepmother blamed her for bringing the message in the first place.

Mist in the hills was a strange thing. It could make the land seem so different, collecting in the hollows and among the trees, and lying in strands on the slopes, allowing shafts of sun, brilliant with dew, to penetrate here and there. Even on familiar ground it was possible to lose your way, or for someone to jump out and surprise you! Beti went steadily on in her clogs, the path being visible for only a few yards ahead. Meanwhile, down below her in the valley a great pall of mist was blanketing the turnpike road, the tollhouse and the ruined gate, keeping the secrets of last night. With nothing to be seen she could almost pretend that nothing had happened. She would keep an eye out for it on the way home though.

The further she got to Tŷ Mawr, the more often the sun broke through on the hills bringing with it the real world and the realisation that there was bound to be much talk at the Big House about what happened last night. Cook would be full of it. Beti would have to be careful of what she said. She was nearing the lodge now but she would not risk going through the main gates this morning. She followed along the high wall of the park towards the little gate which she knew would be left open for her. She went through, bolted the gate and started up the gravel path.

'Beti Roberts!' A voice came hissing through the wall behind taking her by surprise, but after a moment's hesitation she went on, across the kitchen garden.

'Beti. Stop I say! Take a message to Gwilym Roberts!'

Not again! Beti's heart sank. She stood in silence.

'Are you listening now? It was a man's voice all right, but pitched high, as if singing.

'Are you hearing me, Beti Roberts?'

'Aye!'

'Then tell your father this, Beti Roberts. If he or any of his friends pay one further toll at the valley gate they will pay yet more dearly to Rebecca!'

Should she reply? Beti paused and considered. 'Why don't you tell him yourself? Why are you telling me?'

The answer was a while coming through the wall and it shook her.

'The way to a man is through those things he holds dearest to his heart. What better than his daughter to carry Beca's warning!'

The voice continued, gently yet more insistent. 'You see, Beti, in your small way you too are a daughter of Rebecca. You are one of the family of ordinary folk who work all hours that the Lord gave us, to pay our church tithes, our tolls on the gates and our dues to the landlords who get fat on them. Like the one who lives in this grand park! But I tell you, laws can be changed! And we are going to smash and burn those gates until every last one has gone and till those who make the laws stop and listen to us! Now walk on, Beti Roberts, walk on to the fine house! And, oh yes, don't you forget that the grand people who live there eat well because your own brothers and sisters go hungry!'

Numbly, Beti continued towards the house and quickly the anger grew inside her. Anger for what? Because Harri would sometimes eat for breakfast as much as all the little ones put together would get in the whole day! And it did not come easy to admit that poor, spiteful, straggled-haired Gwenno, scrubbing floors in her frayed, patched petticoats, found more love to spare for all her children than Mrs Constance Wynne-Jones, rustling down corridors in her fine silk, could spare for Harri.

27

Before she turned from the kitchen garden towards the servants' entrance at the back, Beti glanced up at the house. It was surely the biggest house for miles around. The porch alone, supported on two marble pillars was higher than the roof of her own home. The walls were so smooth and the slate roof so imposing with its tall chimneys. Pencnwc's walls were rough with *clom* which gave the windows an odd shape and the one chimney was all askew. Tŷ Mawr's long windows looked so elegant, ranged in three neat rows matching each side of the front door. And look, there was Harri staring at her from the window of his room on the first floor, white faced and anxious.

Jenkyn was coming towards her from the back of the house, trailing a hoe across the gravel. 'Master Harri's been a naughty boy,' he said, following Beti's gaze up to the window. 'Out last night, he was, after dark. Had to wake Moses over the stable to let him in. You should have heard the carry on! The house was barred and bolted early last night, see, because of the trouble down below. Heard about it did you?' Her friends studied her face closely.

'Oh, yes.' Beti nodded, trying to sound offhand. 'Did he let on then...I mean, did Harri say where he'd been?'

28

'Not yet. But they'll have it out of him. If they haven't guessed already!'

They both glanced up again at the window. Harri was still staring down.

'Locked in now, he is. Grandad's orders,' Jenkyn explained. 'His Mam'll have him out of there soon enough. Spoils him something terrible!'

Beti saw Harri again later that morning as she struggled across the hall with a bucket full of ashes from the drawing room grate.

'Suppose they're full of it in the back kitchen?' he questioned morosely.

'If you mean about the valley gate, yes.'

'What are they saying? Mother and Grandfather won't even mention it.' He was trying to sound casual but Beti could tell he was really keen to know.

'Lots of things. All sorts.'

Leisa, the cook, had not stopped talking about last night's attack on the gate since she first entered the kitchen, constantly mentioning her husband, Moses, till people might have suspected he had actually been down there! And when Samuel, the gardener, and old Daniels turned up for their morning tea, they had to go through it all over again. Beti had been quite glad when Mrs Wynne-Jones rang down complaining that her fire was not attended to and she was instructed to make haste with the cinder bucket and the black leading. Indeed there was so much excitement in the house many jobs were being neglected.

'I should not be surprised if my Grandfather isn't on the Board of Trustees,' Harri announced grandly and put his head back to push the blond hair out of his eyes. 'They'll have a new gate up there in no time. That'll show them! The rabble!'

'Did you get whipped for going out last night?' Beti retorted angrily, remembering Harri's solemn face at the window.

'What are you talking about! You're the one in trouble. When they find out your father was one of the men attacking the gate he'll be deported to the colonies, somewhere far away like Australia! You'll never see him again. But first they'll make him say who Rebecca really is. You'll be dismissed from your job here and your family will be thrown out of the cottage!'

'Nobody knows who Rebecca is and I never said my Da was there!'

'You don't have to. I saw for myself. I was there watching with you.'

'You couldn't have seen my Da. Why are you so nasty?' In tears now Beti dropped the cinder bucket. Hot coals tumbled across the hall rug. She scrambled after them and blistered her hands returning them to the bucket.

'Stop that howling, for heavens sake! I didn't mean it.'

But Beti could not stop and the noise of her crying brought Mr Wynne-Jones out of his study with a very cross look on his face. He spoke to Harri in English.

'Harri, what is this? Have you nothing better to do than gossip with the servants, keeping them from their work? I would have thought you were in trouble enough already. Off with you now to the library. Find yourself a good book to read.'

'Yes, Grandfather.' Harri's face went bright pink. He screwed up his eyes and slunk away.

'And Beti, what is all this crying for?' asked Mr Wynne-Jones, reverting to Welsh. 'Occupy yourself properly in this house and there should be no time for letting your emotions get out of hand so. I have always understood you to be a good little worker. I hope you will not give me cause to think otherwise.' He considered her very sternly and she trembled to think what might happen now, especially when the scorch marks were discovered on the rug.

'Do I smell burning? Ah, the cinder bucket, of course. I suggest you bring it out onto the terrace before it does damage to my hallway, Beti, and while you compose yourself in the sunshine you can tell me what this has all been about. My grandson says so little of what he

31

has been up to. Such a quiet boy. But I'm sure you must know!'

'Oh dear!' Even though he had been so spiteful Beti never intended to make an enemy of Harri and she certainly did not want to tell tales on him. There was already too much of that sort of thing going on! But how was it to be avoided?

Mr Wynne-Jones seated himself in a cane chair on the terrace. 'Sit on those steps, girl, and tell me first what upset you in the hall just now. I cannot believe that Harri makes a habit of threatening our kitchen maids.'

Beti wiped her eyes, and studying the row of buttons holding together her master's bulging, velvet waistcoat, finally found the courage to speak.

'Nothing, sir.'

'Nonsense! Nobody cries for nothing.' Mr Wynne-Jones shifted his large bulk impatiently in the cane chair, fingered his gold watch chain and crossed and uncrossed his stout legs. 'Come, I'm a busy man. As nice as it is to sit in the sun, I'll not waste my time!'

'The daughters of Rebecca, sir, when they're caught, sir, do they get deported?'

'What an extraordinary question! Why should a kitchen maid concern herself with such matters? From what I hear you had best keep out of it.'

'But Harri said...'

'What has Harri got to do with this?' demanded Mr Wynne-Jones rising to his feet. 'You had better tell me more!'

'Oh no, sir! It's not Harri. It's my father, sir!' There. It was out.

'Your father? Gwilym Roberts? What has he to do with this business?'

'Nothing... nothing until Rebecca sent a message... then he didn't know which way to turn, sir. Last night, if he didn't go, who knows what might have happened. Destroy our cart and all the hay, kill Blod, burn the house down with the little ones inside!'

'Oh, come now! I can hardly believe...' Mr Wynne-Jones paused for a few moments before adding, ominously, 'Your father should know better than to get involved with such people. He would be breaking the law. There are terrible penalties. He should think more of his family.'

At that very moment Nancy, the parlour maid, appeared on the terrace to announce the arrival of two gentlemen from the constabulary to see Mr Wynne-Jones.

'I will see them in the library. Now Beti, I trust you will note what I have said. These matters about which we have just spoken are very grave indeed. Above all I warn you to be careful of everything you say and do. Now

then, Nancy, take this child into the kitchen.
Tell Cook to give her light work. I see she has
sore hands.'

The parlour maid sniffed her disapproval
and in a storm of anxiety Beti picked up the
cinder bucket and followed her to the back of
the house. Cook decided light work was
polishing a mountain of household silver
which was still rough work for Beti's hands
but infinitely better than peeling potatoes or
carrots, and she discovered that the kitchen
door had been left ajar and, by placing herself
at the corner of the scrubbed wooden table,
that she had a view right down the corridor
into the hall.

The first thing she saw was Harri dodging
out of the library and through the front door,
then Nancy conducting Harri's grandfather
into the library. A long time passed, long
enough for Beti to have polished all the knives.
Then the bells began to ring. First Cook was
summoned to the library, then Watcyn, the
manservant and Moses, the coachman, only
just returned from town, then Nancy, then old
Daniels and Samuel, the gardener, together.
Grim faced, in turn, they were all dismissed.
Nobody was saying anything. Cook banged
about more than usual on the stove. Beti
waited her turn. She considered running
home. They were bound to call her. She

34

finished the forks and went on to the spoons. No call came.

When the bell rang again, Beti almost jumped out of her skin, but a quick glance at the board high up on the wall revealed that it was the drawing room bell.

'That'll be the mistress expecting us to feed that wretched kitten. There's no help for it, Beti, you'll have to go. But come to the sink first. You can't go with hands like that.'

Comforting her freshly scrubbed, bright red fingers beneath her apron, Beti was pushed out into the hall just as Mr Wynne-Jones emerged from the library with the two men from the constabulary.

'Well, I did tell you they would know nothing, gentlemen,' murmured Mr Wynne-Jones, in English, as he took them to the door. 'Let us hope something comes to light as you make further enquiries. Ah, Harri! This is my grandson, gentlemen.'

'I don't suppose this young man would have been witness to any of the events last night, sir?'

Just for a moment Harri's face lit up.

'Good heavens. No!' exclaimed his grandfather, wrapping the boy soundly in his arms. 'Harri was tucked up in bed, like every good boy should be!'

4

So much had happened at Tŷ Mawr that day that it would have been no great surprise if, at the end of it, Beti had forgotten there was a message to take home from Rebecca.

'Too late!' shouted Gwilym Roberts when he heard it. 'And you can take this message back to Beca! Caleb Jones and myself, we carted turnips to town this morning. Went by the valley turnpike without paying a penny! Twm Davies was there too, fussing with a piece of chain he had in mind to use in place of the gate. Watched us through. Made out to ask us for the toll money, mind. 'Hey!' he cries with us driving through, past the house but not stopping. Same coming back in the afternoon with lime. Twm, poor dab, doesn't know which way to turn. At least that's what we thought at the time, but somebody reported us!'

'We've had the law here!' Gwenno hissed from the fireside and bumped the baby on her knee. 'The constable came. Your Dad will be summonsed unless he pays the toll. And he must swear to pay his dues on the gate every time!'

'But Rebecca says . . .!'

'I know what Rebecca says!' roared Gwilym, rising from his chair in fury and lashing out at Beti with his elbow. She went reeling into the wall, knocking everything flying as she went down on the floor.

The little ones gathered in a huddle round her. Things could not be worse. She had nothing in the basket for them. For a while they whispered and tugged at the basket but soon even they sensed that tonight was a night without any comfort at all. And all Beti could think was if only she had been allowed time to explain to Mr Wynne-Jones that it was because they were so poor, so little money to pay for going through that gate, to get food and clothes for the little ones, to stop Gwenno worrying about the workhouse, Mr Wynne-Jones might have put things right.

Then she saw Gwenno drag a piece of paper from under her chair. 'Look at this, baby. The constable left it. It's a proclamation in English from Queen Victoria, far away in London. I told him nobody here can read, but he said he'd leave it to remind us that there's a five hundred pound reward for anyone who splits on Rebecca!'

Gwilym Roberts sat with his face to the wall. Gwenno, putting her head back now and then to laugh silently, went on whispering to the baby.

'The workhouse. The workhouse. That's where we'll be before the week is out. There's only one good thing about the workhouse. I'll

37

be kept apart from my useless husband! La, La!'

Then came a tapping at the window.

'It's the parish constable to take us to the workhouse!' cried her stepmother.

'Lord save us!' muttered Gwilym. 'What now?' Then they all sat in frozen silence, even the baby, for there was no telling just how many people were out there in the darkness. Without leaving his chair Gwilym reached stealthily for the stout stick he kept by the hearth.

Then came a tapping at the door. 'Mrs Roberts! Mrs Roberts!' It was only Watcyn from the Big House with the news that Siân Jones who did the washing at Tŷ Mawr had slipped on some stone flags and hurt her arm. Would Mrs Roberts come early in the morning to wash for Tŷ Mawr?

'Me?' asked Gwenno, amazed. She had never before done washing at the Big House.

'Yes, indeed, Mrs Wynne-Jones asked for you, specially.'

Gwenno looked very flustered and turned to her husband.

'You should go,' he said, but without enthusiasm.

'The children?'

'Oh, no,' said the man who had edged his way out of the night into the cottage. 'Mrs Wynne-

Jones will not allow the children. It is suggested that Beti stays here with them.'

This seemed to please Gwenno. Beti pushed the children off and got to her feet. This was not fair. It was she who worked at the Big House, not her stepmother.

It was to be a gloomy household Gwenno left behind her early next morning. Beti lay on her back bruised and sullen but wide awake on the big feather mattress, and the children watched from the loft as their mother went through her preparations to leave.

'Don't know what you've got to sing about,' Beti heard her father remark.

'Answer to my prayers. That's what it is, Gwilym. I knew He'd answer me in the end!'

'Huh. What have you got to pray for?'

'A chance to get out of this place, free of the children for once, free of people coming here telling us what to do, what not to do! Rebecca! Who knows, up at the Big House I might speak to someone, influence things. Get us out of this mess!'

'Woman, you're going to the wash house. You won't set foot in Tŷ Mawr. The wash house is way across the yard. Beti could tell you. You'll be too busy up to your arms in soap and scrubbing!'

'That's what you think!'

Beti heard the latch lifted on the door and Gwilym said his last words to his wife before she set out on the dawn walk to the Big House.

'Calling you like this to Tŷ Mawr is not by chance, Gwenno. Don't go thinking that for one minute. And I warn you. Mind what you say! There's more to it than we know and it makes me nervous!'

'Everything makes you nervous!'

Whether there was more to it or not Gwenno was back home again in the afternoon with money.

'A whole shilling! Extra for the inconvenience and turning out so prompt as I did,' she repeated with pride.

'And because we've lost my wages today,' Beti reminded her.

'Could be,' her stepmother agreed sourly. 'But they will almost certainly want me again. As it happens there wasn't that much washing to do today, there being no guests at the house. That's how I got away early. And a good drying day, of course! I dashed back with the money so you can take it into town for me. It'll pay for Gwilym's toll. You're to go to the Courthouse, Beti. You'll have to ask. Anyone in town will tell you where to find it. And when you get there, say the money's on behalf of Gwilym Roberts of Pencnwc, with his humblest apologies.'

'I don't think...'

'You don't think what, Beti? You do not think your father would want us to be paying this toll? Well, that's too bad. I'm not having us breaking the law, treated as criminals. Certainly not now I'm employed at the Big House!'

'Well, I shan't go!' Beti especially resented her stepmother's intrusion into Tŷ Mawr.

'You will go, my lady! Or I shall tell Mrs Wynne-Jones next time I see her that you will not be going to the Big House again, not ever! I shall have to explain to her that things have got to change. She will understand.'

Beti pictured elegant Mrs Constance Wynne-Jones with her fair ringlets, her lace, her rings and her satin slippers and she knew in her own mind that such a conversation with dark, drab, weary Gwenno could not take place. But could she risk it?

Beti also recognised that a new side to Gwenno had come to light and perhaps things would never be the same again.

'As I said, you'll go with the money to the Courthouse and I shall deal with your father.'

5

Going to town, especially to the Courthouse, meant putting on her one good gown and best shawl and the bonnet reserved for Sundays. Gwenno retrieved them from the clothes press, shook them out and stood over Beti, anxious to button and tie her into them as quickly as possible.

'You'll wear my boots,' Gwenno insisted, 'So you can hide the shilling inside.'

The boots were too big of course and the little ones laughed at her but she knew better than to argue with Gwenno in this mood.

'Let me look at you,' said her stepmother, bundling Beti round. 'Well, you'll have to do. I won't have any folk giving you a ride on their cart saying Gwenno Roberts doesn't know how to dress her family.'

'I won't be going on any cart. I'm walking.'

'You'll do as I say and go by the turnpike road! Walking's too long. Besides I want people to notice you. And when you get offered a ride with anyone you make sure you tell them why you're going into town!'

Beti stamped to the door in her uncomfortable boots.

'Don't you misbehave with me, girl!' Gwenno followed her, shouting: 'Down that hill with you!' She watched Beti struggling down the path to the turnpike road. 'You brought Rebecca into this house! You can take the shilling!'

Beti was not going to pay that shilling! She'd go along the road for a while then she'd turn back. Her father would never forgive her if she paid. The first vehicle to come along was a cart, top-heavy with hay. Beti recognised poor John Phillips who had to take his load through the tollgate, from his fields on one side, to his hayguard on the other side. He had an angry, determined look on him. Beti felt sure he would not be paying his toll. He'd probably been there when they destroyed the gate.

'Jump up, Beti. How far you going?'

'Just to the Big House,' she lied. 'Prefer to walk, thank you, Mr Phillips.'

The farmer looked surprised, noted her best Sunday clothes and went on towards the tollhouse. From up on the hill Gwenno's voice came shrieking down, but so cross that Beti couldn't make out the words. She walked on and soon heard the clipping of hooves on the stoney road. Coming up behind her was a strange donkey and cart and on it a curious old man.

'Will you be wanting a ride, dearie?' The old man had radiant blue eyes set in a wrinkled, brown face. He spoke in soft English which was different from anything she had heard before. He smiled broadly and to Beti's surprise at the same time the shaggy, brown-eyed donkey turned his big head and bared his teeth in a grin.

'I'm going West, dearie. Come to think of it, I've been going West ever since I started out weeks ago. Brecon, Llandovery, Llandeilo, Carmarthen, Haverfordwest. Can you get more West than that, now?'

The old man put out a gnarled hand and before she knew it Beti was being hauled up to sit beside him in the little cart, laden with bales of cloth and bundles of linen.

'We'll be off then, shall we?' He clucked to his donkey and they rumbled on. 'Padraic the Pedlar, that's me. Elijah and me have a fine load of linen and lace from the port of Bristol. We're doing the round trip again, through the fairs and markets, selling to the good Welsh folk, and we'll maybe buy up some of their flannel. And then we'll be taking ship from Tenby back to the city. Now, Elijah enjoys his sea voyage, don't you, old fellow?'

Elijah, the donkey, picked his way through the bigger stones, the ruts and the holes. There was no telling if he liked the sea. Beti could not say either. She had never seen the sea.

'Now, sometimes, instead of going back to Bristol, we cross home to Ireland, to see me dear old mother,' continued Padraic, 'It depends. In fact it depends on a lot of things whether I come this way again. For instance, there's been terrible tales of violence in these parts. In fact I've seen evidence of it with my own eyes. Terrible things done in the dead of night, I'm told.'

They rounded a bend in the road and there before them was the scorched tollhouse.

'There you are! Will you just look at that! Terrible! Who would have done such a thing? Look at that poor man, now, coming out from that place!'

Twm Tollgate had a desperate look on his face. The chain he had fixed across the road in place of the gate was now dragging in pieces on the ground. He seemed not to recognise Beti in her Sunday clothes and made a big fuss of measuring the width of the pedlar's cart.

'Sure, it's two pence. What I paid last time,' insisted the old man. 'I was through here only last Michaelmas!'

Twm set his face hard. 'It's gone up since then, boy. Three pence at least, by my calculations.'

'The Devil it has! It's a wicked old world,' grumbled Padraic, searching for his pennies in a leather bag hanging from his waist. 'There! I'll not be coming this way again, if I can help it! And me saying what a poor fellow you was!

Full of sympathy I was for your poor house and your gate gone. You'll not be deserving it.'

Twm Tollgate sighed. 'I don't make the rules, boy, I just take the money and pass it on.'

'Sure. They all say that! Walk on, Elijah. Walk on!'

The old pedlar had given Beti new heart. Now she felt brave and cheerful. 'We'll be passing a farm before very long. Drop me there, if you please. I'm on a message for my mother.'

'Take care now, dearie!' Padraic urged as Elijah drew the cart to a halt at the next farm gate. 'There's bad people about in these parts. They tell me the women are the worst. A word of advice, now. Don't trust a woman specially if she's called Rebecca!'

Beti thanked the pedlar and waited until his cart had trundled out of sight before heading across the road into a willow copse where she found a mossy mound beside a stream and began to struggle with her stepmother's uncomfortable boots. She would make better progress across the fields in her bare feet. Besides, she wanted to check on the shilling. It tumbled out at the edge of the water. It was a new shilling. Even in the shade it was silvery bright.

'A shilling for the gate! Eh, Missie?' A big hand shot out and grabbed the shilling and another clamped across her mouth. She was rolled over and over at the edge of the stream and pushed down into the moist earth. She lost her bonnet and her shawl was torn off and wrapped round her head.

6

Beti lay in a darkened place, bruised and sore. Now she knew just what it was like to be a sack of flour humped on the miller's shoulders and thrown on the back of the farmer's horse to make the bumping journey home from the millhouse!

The shilling was still with her, thrown on the dusty floor where two men had bundled her. She had heard one of them trying it in his teeth and insisting, as they carried her away struggling, that the shilling should be their's to keep.

'We'll not take money ill-gotten, paid to Gwenno Roberts to cheat Rebecca!' his companion shouted.

'And why should Beti Roberts have it? By rights that shilling should go to the cause,' continued the young man, riding the mare alongside her.

'I'll none of it. T'is blood money! Hold that girl!'

They were climbing now, up into the rough scrub-covered slopes. Beti, more uncomfortable than ever, slung over the back of the jolting cob, with her hands and feet brushing the bushes, began calling out.

'Stop that, now!' A firm hand came down on her head, pushing her face into the horse's flank. 'Jiw, I hope we did right. I see trouble with this one,' the young man grumbled. 'Take her with us tonight, is it? Let them see we mean business! When Beca says no paying at the gate, by heaven, Beca means it!'

'So!' Beti considered miserably. 'I'm to be a hostage! They'll take me with them to burn some gate out in the country and then I'll be in real trouble with everyone! These people will make me do things I don't want to do. I'll be dismissed from the Big House!'

From that time on she was too upset to pay heed of where they were taking her. At last the horses came to a halt. She heard a door latch raised and her feet scraped a stone wall. Then they were trotting briskly and in silence over smooth ground and soon they stopped again and she was dragged off the horse and hurried into a building. There they removed her shawl. She was in a kind of barn and in the gloom was confronted by two men in cloaks and masks.

48

They pushed her, still bound, onto a pile of old sacks in a corner.

'Stay quiet and you'll come to no harm.' The man was disguising his voice behind his hand.

'Can I . . .'

'Quiet, girl!'

Outside dusk was descending behind the tiny windows. Beti looked around quickly, taking in as much as she could of the dirty, cobwebby workman's hut, full of pots and tools and dangerous things like scythes and axes.

'We'll rest now, for a while,' said the older man, clearing a space amongst the clutter. 'Close the shutters, boy. Then padlock the door.'

'Time enough for a kip before the fun starts, eh?' said the other as they settled down.

Beti, could only shuffle closer into the sacks for comfort and as the men whispered in the darkness, into her tired mind drifted the kitchen in Pencnwc with Gwenno rocking baby at the hearth and the little ones up on the bench, their tangled heads pressed against the window, watching for her coming with her basket.

'Not tonight,' sobbed Beti. 'Not tonight!' and she drifted into sleep.

How much later was it when she awoke? There was no way of telling, but there were sounds in the room and a chink of moonlight coming through the shutters showed the two men moving about.

'You're standing on my skirt.'

'Where's that bonnet?' came the retort.

'Never mind! Hurry! Hurry! Fetch the horses.'

'Pass that shawl, then!'

The door opened and one man stepped out into the night, leaving for just a second, a broad figure framed in the moonlight, fumbling with bonnet strings. The daughters of Rebecca! Beti shivered as chill night air swept in.

When he was back with the horses one of the men made a dart towards her. 'Come on then, my lovely.'

'Leave her!'

'Come on. We're taking her with us. She rides behind me!'

'I told you, leave her. This is an ugly, dangerous business. I'll not involve young girls!'

'Thought we were all girls together!'

'This is no time for jokes,' growled the other man. 'Come! Let's be off!'

7

The two men and their horses slipped away into the night, leaving Beti still trussed up. She had seen just briefly the shilling, shining on the earth floor, caught in the moonlight before the door closed on her, and she was reminded then how the windows of Pencnwc would shine on a moonlit night to guide her home. What she would give now to be trotting free along the silvery path across the hills towards Pencnwc! When would she see home again? When would she be back safe in the kitchen of Tŷ Mawr? Slicing turnips, cleaning boots, carrying cinders, anything would be better than this! Surely by now they would be missing her at home! Gwenno would have some explaining to do.

Then suddenly outside came the sound of someone running up to the door and struggling with the lock. They had come back for her. She was to go with them to the gate after all! The door flew open, the gardener's boy hurtled in and Beti's heart burst with relief.

'Jenkyn!'

He swung his lantern into her face. 'Beti! What are you doing here?'

'Jenkyn, untie me. Please untie me!'

Her friend hesitated for a moment, so surprised was he to see her there but at last he took a knife from his belt and slit the cords which bound her.

'Jiw! How d'you get in here, girl? Cook said you was minding the kids today. Look at you, all dressed up.'

Beti struggled to her feet and brushed past Jenkyn. 'Where's this place?' she demanded, looking out into the night.

'My father's shed, of course.'

'The gardener's shed, part of the Big House?'

'What's going on, Beti?'

'Nothing.' She just did not know if she could trust Jenkyn.

'Nothing! And you locked in here and tied up! You mean you won't tell me, and I've just saved you! I thought we were friends. What's this?' Jenkyn's lantern shone down on the shilling.

'Mine. It's mine!'

'How d'you come by that, Beti.'

'Never you mind! I'm getting out of here.' Beti grabbed the shilling and discovered Gwenno's boots close by.

'Know the way, do you? Reckon you'll have to come with me. Only ran back for this for my father. He'll be waiting!' Jenkyn reached for an axe which hung with its steely head embedded in a beam. 'You coming?'

Given barely time to think Beti slung Gwenno's boots round her neck and went with him. It was a struggle for Beti to keep pace as Jenkyn sped across moonlit lawns and down shadowy tree-lined ways.

'Watch out!' he hissed, holding the lantern high as they skirted the edge of an ornamental pond. It was all growing familiar. They were getting closer to the Big House, and now and then they caught sight of lights blazing out from its great windows. As they ran behind the yew hedge which separated the park from the kitchen garden the lantern almost fluttered out several times, but they could now hear voices and suddenly they were in a clearing lit by flaming brands and packed with a milling host on horseback. There was an anxious buzz in the air, a mixture of muffled voices and the sound of horses snorting and pawing the cobbles. The yard of the home farm, thought Beti, as she studied the shadows dancing on the surrounding walls and the people coming and going through darkened doorways.

They were crouching at the side of a hayrick. 'You stay put', Jenkyn instructed. 'I'll have to look for my father and give him this.' He waved the axe high and its blade reflected blood red and gold in the torchlight. 'I'll be back, don't fret. My father'll not let me ride tonight!'

There were already many weapons among the crowd, stakes and clubs and axes, which

Beti noticed as she watched Jenkyn pushing among them. It seemed they had arrived not a moment too soon, for suddenly a voice boomed out and a hush fell on the yard.

'Come now, my daughters! Let us bring fire and destruction to the Turnpike Trusts. Let us make it a night never to be forgotten in this valley! Away, my daughters! Away!'

Rebecca's voice rang out deep and full of threat. One man riding high in his stirrups, rose up in the middle of the crowd dressed in bonnet and shawl and petticoats, and waved his companions forward. With a muted cheer they clattered through the yard and passed out into the night, leaving behind a solitary figure with a lantern against the darkness—Jenkyn.

'You'll be off home now then?' he called.

Beti yawned and realised she was very tired indeed. She was uncomfortable too in her best gown, which was by now all stained and crumpled. How could she go home like that in the middle of the night?

'I can't!'

'Can't? Just what have you been up to that you can't talk about?'

'I can't go home!'

'Fraid of the dark, is it?'

'Don't be silly! I've walked home ever so many times in the dark.' A man's cry in the distance reminded her of what was soon to happen. Some tollkeeper and his family at the far end of the valley were certainly not likely to forget this night.

'What then?'

'My Da will be so angry, Jenkyn,' Beti sniffed.

'Look, if you promise to tell me tomorrow what this is all about, I'll show you a place where you can sleep in Tŷ Mawr.

'The Big House! Oh no!'

'Quite safe, girl. At the very top. No one's going to know. Special way in only I know about. Come on!' Jenkyn grabbed her hand and pulled her through the kitchen garden and down a path between some buildings.

'Here we are!' They were up against the rear wall of the house. Jenkyn shone his light on a low plank door. One shove with his foot and it creaked open.

'Go on, Beti.' He pushed her through. Inside the air was chill and musty and she discovered she was in a passage running behind the dairy. Why had she never noticed this tiny door before? Jenkyn dowsed his lantern. 'Come on!' Beti followed him past familiar rooms—the scullery, the pantry, the kitchen, all with moonlight streaming in, until they reached the foot of the servants' stairs where a cat jumped out at them.

'Hush. It's only Mog!' Jenkyn pulled her

with him up the stairs, up, up, one, two, three flights.

Beti knew that Nancy had her room in the attic, probably Watcyn too. She had been up there only once before in her life, to fetch baby clothes from a store room, clothes that the mistress had said she could take home when Catrin was born. At that time Gwenno had wanted to call the baby Constance after Mrs Wynne-Jones, but Gwilym would not have it.

Jenkyn was opening a door, ever so quietly. 'There!' By the light of the moon she saw a bed set against the wall. 'See you in the morning!' he muttered.

8

This was the first night Beti had ever spent away from home, the first night she had not slept in the loft since she was a baby being rocked in the cradle by Sarah, her real mother, before she died. She nevertheless slumbered heavily through the remaining hours of darkness, undisturbed and unaware of whatever comings and goings there might be outside.

Then, as dawn was breaking, she awoke to hear Nancy hurrying down to make breakfast.

Beti jumped out of bed, quickly pulled on her gown, tidied herself as best she could and left the room, deciding that if she went down the front stairs there would be less chance of meeting anyone so early in the morning.

She was wrong. Harri was just coming out of his room, looking smug and clutching a telescope.

'What were you doing up there, Beti Roberts? Have you been in the attic? Look at your clothes all crumpled.'

Beti pushed past him without a word.

'Not telling? All right. I'll find out. I shall report the matter to my grandfather and to my mother. You'll have to explain to them. Stupid girl!'

Then he started to push her down the stairs. 'They'll need you in the kitchen. We're having breakfast early because we're all off to the Courthouse. Your father's up before the magistrate.'

Beti stopped at once and took the full weight of Harri's thrust in her back.

'Didn't you know?' he joked. 'Didn't you know your father's in court today?'

'For what?' Beti forced a whisper.

'Oh, come off it! Refusing to pay the tolls. And worse than that, I suspect!' Now he was trying to sound just like his grandfather.

'What sort of worse?' She was doing her best to seem unconcerned.

'How should I know?' Harri retorted flippantly. 'At the very least he'll be deported to the colonies!'

'Harri!' Mrs Wynne-Jones was calling her son from the landing below. 'Come down at once, Harri. I wish to see if you are dressed properly for going out.'

He ran down stairs three at a time leaving Beti to follow hesitantly.

'I suppose it will have to do, although I would have preferred you in that brown suit, Harri. Now, I expect you to behave yourself in court. Otherwise.... Why, Beti Roberts! What are you doing on the front stairs at this time of day? And where is your apron...'

'Can I go to the Courthouse, Ma'am?' Beti implored in her rough English, for Mrs Wynne-Jones spoke no Welsh.

'The Courthouse? You? Good gracious me, no. It's no place for you!'

'But it's so important. It's my father.'

'If your father is in some kind of trouble the least you know about it the better!' insisted her mistress. 'Besides, I would very much doubt if Cook can spare you. We have a large party here for lunch. There will be plenty of vegetables for you to clean,' and clutching her wide, blue satin skirts she swept on down to the hall.

Oh the injustice of it! Harri would go to the court. He would see her father but she wouldn't. Was anything so unfair?. Beti crept on down the stairs. The front door stood wide open. She looked out into the sunny garden with its bright, tidy borders and the neat avenue of elms and the gravel drive stretching right up to the distant main gates.

Perhaps I should run home this very minute, thought Beti. Perhaps Gwenno would be expecting me. No! She'd want to know why the toll was not paid. So where's the shilling? she'd say. 'The shilling! Jiw! I've left it in the boots upstairs!'

'Beti! That you? Come on, girl!'

'I'm going to fetch something from upstairs, Cook.'

'Oh no, Miss, you'll come in here at once and get on with these jobs in my kitchen!

Harri was hovering about. 'I'll go. In the attic is it?'

In dismay Beti watched him bound up the stairs. He must have quessed where she had been. She knew he would find the boots. Miserably she entered the kitchen where on the table a mountain of vegetables awaited her, potatoes, carrots, turnips, beans.

'I see we're in our best today,' Cook

remarked at once. 'Well, you can think again if you're preparing for a trip to the Courthouse. You won't be let out of this kitchen today, my girl. They'll all be back here for lunch before you can say Rebecca!'

She rolled her sleeves up her fat arms and began dredging the table with flour. 'Best gown or no, I want these black currants picked over and washed here and now. We'll get the tarts done first. What is that mother of yours thinking of, sending you to work in the kitchen dressed like that? Ideas above her station just because she's done the washing once for the Big House! Well, she won't be coming back here in a hurry. Siân is due back today and there's a big wash, more than Gwenno Roberts could cope with. Just look at your feet! Where's your clogs, for heaven's sake? Go get yourself a pair. There's some spare in the wash house. And quickly!'

That was how Beti came to glimpse the huge pile of white sheets hidden in big baskets behind the copper in the wash house. Extra grimy they were too, more than you'd expect for bed linen in a grand house. And chancing a quick snoop round she also discovered caps and petticoats in a closed chest, and not the type that the fine lady of the house would wear. She understood now what Cook meant when she said it was more than Gwenno Roberts could cope with!

As she hurried back across the yard, she spotted Jenkyn with his father. Samuel had his son by the shoulders and was shouting at him. She was sure she heard her own name and they both turned abruptly when they noticed her passing. Secrets! Beti was sorry that she and Jenkyn were divided by their secrets. She really did want someone to talk to.

Cook, engrossed and cheerful in her pastry making, now spoke to her more kindly. 'Get your apron, child. And don't you worry now about your Da. I tell you things have a habit of turning out for the best.'

For the best! As Cook hummed her way through six black currant lattice tarts, Beti took up a knife and attacked the vegetables. This for the magistrate! she vowed, stabbing the eye of the first fat potato. And, oh yes, this for Rebecca!

As she peeled and scraped the raw skins, Beti recalled what she had been told of the merciless life in the colonies, and pictured her father, chained in a gang, breaking his back under the blistering sun. As she broke open the pods and let the beans burst out noisily into the bowl, she thought of the little ones, locked in the workhouse, made to be thankful by the stern and ever watchful, parish guardian for bowls of thin broth served in cold, dark rooms where the sun never reached through the high windows, when all they wanted was to play and run free on the hills. Not much to ask. And it wasn't their fault that they were so poor. If only she'd had a chance to explain this to Mr Wynne-Jones...

'Come on now, Beti. Don't cry so. Look, I've made you this.' Cook put a tiny currant turnover on the table by Beti's elbow and of course, it was then she realised just how hungry she was, having eaten nothing since the previous morning.

Cook put the vegetables on to boil and Beti just did not know whether to be glad or sorry that the time was approaching for the visitors to arrive. She wanted desperately to know what had happened in the court and yet she feared to know.

She began listening for every possible sound of carriages on the forecourt, doors opening, voices carrying down the hall, shouts of welcome. Time and again she found reason to go to a window. The waiting became almost intolerable. Then Gwenno came back into her mind, Gwenno sitting at home in the cottage, whispering her wild fears of the workhouse to her children.

'Perhaps I should have run home, anyway,'

she found herself telling Cook as she stirred a pan of junket over the fire.

'Hush! I do believe I can hear something. Yes. I knew they would hardly be late with Mr Wynne-Jones presiding at the court.'

There was indeed a distant rumble and soon the very definite scrape of carriage wheels on gravel.

'Beti!' Cook's stern voice rang out but too late. Beti was through the door and racing the length of the hall. She landed against a window beside the front door which Watcyn was hastening to open.

'Get away from there, girl!' he hissed but she would not move.

Four carriages had already arrived and more were approaching down the drive. Out of nowhere came Samuel, running to clear something from the foot of the steps. Gwenno's boots! Beti watched in horror. How did they get there? Harri! Harri must have found them and thrown them from the attic window. And where was the shilling?

Watcyn was busy now, helping the ladies from their carriages and into the hall. Oh, so bright, so full of fun! The ladies, chattering in their alien English, breezed past her in crimson, amber, rose and russet gowns, bonnets frilled with lace and satin ribbons.

The gentlemen, following with Mr Wynne-Jones, so tidy in their dark frock coats.

Beti's heart was near to bursting. They had all been at the court. They looked so happy. Surely nothing bad could have happened? Harri would know. Where was Harri? She looked about wildly for Harri. Then she saw him outside, admiring the carriages, and suddenly she saw him stoop and pick something up from the gravel, a round, shiny piece of silver, her shilling! He looked round quickly but did not notice Jenkyn watching him and as he dropped it into his pocket the gardener's boy pounced on him and dragged him into the bushes. No one saw but Beti. The servants were rushing to and fro and guests were chattering wildly in the hall, all too busy to notice the leaves flying and branches cracking as the front door closed on Harri and Jenkyn scrapping in the undergrowth.

Harri's mother was ushering her guests into the dining room.

'Mr Wynne-Jones!' boomed a large and grand lady lingering in the hall, 'I simply must congratulate you! That fellow, Gwilym Roberts! Your judgment was so correct. But all those children! How they are to manage, I cannot imagine!'

Outside yet another carriage was pulling up. Mr Wynne-Jones bowed deeply. 'Madam, I am

convinced things will improve from now on. Pray excuse me!' He started back down the hall, looking very stern. Beti was now convinced the news was bad.

'Where is Watcyn to open this door?' her master demanded. 'Good Lord!' What is happening out there, Beti? Tell me please!'

She joined him as he opened the door himself and she expected to see the two boys still fighting in front of a carriage full of guests.

There was certainly a vehicle out there, but it was a wagon full of people she knew, laughing and waving to her! Gwilym in the front, and Gwenno with Catrin and all the little ones!

Mr Wynne-Jones helped Beti to climb up among them. 'Not one bit of good sending your father to Australia when there's all these to feed, eh Beti? Now it's more clear to me what a problem we have here. People like me will have to see if we can't get a few things changed. We'll sort out these tithes and tolls before long, don't you worry, Gwilym Roberts. Now take your family off home for the rest of the day!'

Gwilym set Blod at a merry pace down the drive. Gwenno kissed Beti and the little ones clambered all over her. As they reached the main gates a boy stepped out in their path. Jenkyn! He was smiling and holding out the shilling for Beti. Beti took it and gave it to Gwenno and Gwenno said: 'Jump up here with us, Jenkyn. We're going home to Pencnwc. The Master says the tolls are going to get sorted out, so we'll pay as we go through the gate this time! And if there's anything left from the shilling we'll have ourselves a feast!'